T0068178

THE CRUISE DETECTIVES

THE CRUISE DETECTIVES

FRED CERRATO

THE CRUISE DETECTIVES

iUniverse books may be ordered through booksellers or by contacting:

iUniverse
1663 Liberty Drive
Bloomington, IN 47403
www.iuniverse.com
844-349-9409

ISBN: 978-1-6632-5650-8 (sc)
ISBN: 978-1-6632-5651-5 (e)

Library of Congress Control Number: 2023918028

Print information available on the last page.

iUniverse rev. date: 09/19/2023

CHAPTER 1

Dave Christos was a private detective from Burlington, Vermont. After graduating from the University of Vermont with a bachelor's degree in liberal arts and with no idea what direction his professional life would take, he decided to follow in his father's footsteps by joining the field of law enforcement. Dave's father, Pete, used to be a police detective at the Detective Services Bureau in Burlington. Many years ago, he had become very famous for solving a murder case in nearby Castleport. Castle College's basketball team had become involved in a point-shaving scandal. Harry Casey, a barber in Burlington, was part of a syndicate that fixed college games. Nat Parro, a player at Castle College, fed Casey information about the team's strategies that could impact the games' outcomes. Casey then fed this information back to the syndicate, which helped them set up betting lines and point spreads. When Casey thought Parro was going to rat to the police about the syndicate, he had one of his henchmen, Remy Calvet, murder the player. Within several days, Pete broke the case wide open and became an instant celebrity. He was interviewed on radio and television, and the *Burlington Free Journal* ran an in-depth article in their Sunday rotogravure section about how he'd solved the crime.

After thirty years of working for the Burlington Police Department, Pete decided to retire and receive his pension. However, he did not want to retire from police work completely, so he opened Christos's Detective Agency on the second floor of 25 Church Street in Burlington Center. He recruited Dave, and the duo built up a healthy clientele with their effective detective work and the help of Pete's notoriety. After fifteen years, the agency was well known in northern and central Vermont and throughout much of New England. With forty-five years of police work under his belt, Pete decided to let Dave do the bulk of the work at the agency. Dave ran the office with his secretary, Diane, and Pete became more of an advisor.

However, even retired, Pete never cleaned up his act. His physical appearance was in shambles forty-five years ago, and it was still in shambles. His wife, Lucia, always tried to help him, but it was to no avail. Wherever he went, Pete could be seen wearing a rumpled suit with a wrinkled white shirt and an askew tie. His wing-tipped shoes were scuffed, and his thinning gray hair was plastered down with Brylcreem. He wore a beard made of three-day-old stubble because he was too lazy to shave. After three days, his beard would itch, and he would trim it with his electric shaver. He was one of the few people who still smoked a pipe. He would try to keep the bowl lit for most of the day. The pleasant aroma of his apple-scented tobacco would waft after him as he sat in his comfortable leather office chair and advised his son.

In contrast to his father, Dave Christos was an Adonis. He had jet-black hair that was always perfectly coiffed. He had piercing blue eyes and a beautifully proportioned face. At six feet two, he had an athlete's body that he kept in shape by lifting weights at a Burlington gym. He enjoyed jogging, but the punishing Vermont winters mostly kept him mostly on the treadmill. The wind howling off Lake Champlain and the blowing snow would often result in wind chill temperatures that were below zero.

If Dave was an Adonis, his wife, Camille, was Aphrodite. She was a green-eyed, blonde French Canadian from Mirabel, a suburb of Montreal. She and Dave had met as students at the University of Vermont, where they'd dated and fallen in love. She kept in shape by jogging when the weather allowed it and cross-country skiing in the winter, which lasted seven months in Vermont. Camille worked with her mother-in-law, Lucia, at Christos's Travel and had done so for many years. Lucia had opened the travel agency on the ground floor of 25 Church Street while Pete was still a police detective. Camille eventually became Lucia's partner, and their business was a great success. They got a lot of traffic, especially in winter, when Vermonters longed for warmer climes to escape the subfreezing temperatures.

Camille and Lucia would earn points from other travel companies because of their high sales, resulting in free trips and cruises. They would close their office for several days and take advantage of these free junkets, oftentimes with their husbands. As a result, they all became world travelers and visited their ancestral countries. Lucia visited Rome, Florence, Naples, and the Amalfi Coast. Pete visited Santorini and the Acropolis in Athens. Camille visited the Louvre and Eiffel Tower in Paris. However, what they loved to do most of all was to cruise. Camille and Lucia always told their clients that a cruise had one of the best values in the travel industry. Once you paid for your cruise, everything except alcoholic drinks was included. One had access to pools, casinos, nightly shows of all types, dancing, and fantastic food that was available at any time of the day or night. You could preplan an excursion, and the cruise line would safely take you to your destination on a modern bus with a professional tour guide. You didn't have to worry about lugging your luggage from hotel to hotel; it was safely stored in your stateroom on the ship.

Camille, Lucia, Dave, and Pete had been on cruises with most of the lines, but their favorite was Sea Atlantic. They thought the accommodations and food on Sea Atlantic ships were the best. They had lost count of how many times they had been on Sea Atlantic cruises. They now had free laundry twice a week and free Wi-Fi for the entire trip. Lucia had even become acquainted with many of the ships' captains due to her attendance at many cocktail receptions. But what they especially liked about the cruises were the casinos.

They all loved to gamble. Lucia and Camille enjoyed the slot machines, and Dave and Pete liked the card games and roulette. All four would often drive for two hours and book themselves into the InterContinental Montreal for the weekend. They would visit the Casino de Montreal on Notre Dame Island, gamble all weekend, and enjoy the fine French-Canadian cuisine.

Pete and Lucia's fortieth wedding anniversary was soon approaching, and Dave and Camille were treating them to a celebratory anniversary cruise on the Sea Atlantic's *Acme*. All the arrangements had been made at the travel agency. This was not a freebie, so Dave and Camille made sure to schedule the ultimate accommodations. They booked adjoining suites on the *Acme* and first-class tickets on a flight to Fort Lauderdale, where they would embark on their cruise. They would fly down the day before the cruise, stay at the Hilton in Fort Lauderdale, and then take the hotel shuttle to the ship the next day.

Phillip Santos was a native of the Philippines who graduated from Quezon City University with a degree in hotel management. His native language was Tagalog, but he was fluent in English, because it was taught in schools and was the country's official language in mass media, art, social interactions, business, and politics. Phillip found it difficult to get a job in the highly urbanized Quezon area. He was young, and the prospect of traveling and working at the same time drew him to the cruise industry. His degree in hotel management and his fluency in English were perfect qualifications, so he was able to get a job with Sea Atlantic, where he became a very popular waiter. He was always upbeat and would entertain the patrons at breakfast while cleaning tables and serving coffee and tea.

In a loud voice, he would announce, "This is Phillip. I hope you have a fabulous day. The sun is shining, and the sky is azure blue." Then he would start singing. "Blue skies smiling at me. Nothing but blue skies do I see." He would sing the entire song in a beautiful baritone voice. When he finished, the surrounding patrons would erupt in applause. He did this every morning and was rewarded with generous tips when the patrons completed their cruises.

Phillip loved the travel afforded to him by the cruise line. At most ports, the workers were allowed to leave the ship and sightsee for an allotted number of hours. But after several years, there were aspects of the job that were becoming unpalatable. The hours were grueling. He worked twelve hours per day, seven days a week. He received a paltry salary of $2,000 per month, and his accommodations below deck were unsatisfactory. His room was a ten-by-ten-foot cube that he shared with a fellow Filipino, Donald Cruz. Phillip's contract lasted for six months. When his contract was over, he got to return home for a sixty-day vacation. Then he would get a new assignment. Phillip could not request where he would go on his new assignment; the company told him. He could end up anywhere in the world: the Mediterranean, the Baltic, Scandinavia, Eastern Europe, or anywhere else.

Phillip was becoming a world traveler, but the meager pay and inferior living conditions were depressing him. He'd begun to think about exploring different opportunities when he learned of a new electronic development by a computer-savvy friend of his. This new electronic development was astonishing, and it changed Phillip's attitude completely. His friend wanted Phillip to test the new technology when he returned to the ship. This new development would make Phillip a very rich man when he went back for his new assignment.

CHAPTER 2

Lucia and Pete lived in a sprawling ranch house in the southern part of Burlington. They had two cars: Lucia's Subaru Forester and Pete's Lincoln Corsair. Both had all-wheel drive to navigate the snowy winter. They were packing for their celebratory ten-day anniversary cruise. An Uber was scheduled to pick them up in an hour and drive them the short distance to Burlington International Airport, where they would meet Camille and Dave. Lucia and Pete packed separately, but Lucia made sure Pete was taking clothes that were ironed and tailored. She wanted Pete to be presentable when they went to dinner, a show, or the casino. She didn't want his lax grooming habits to embarrass them. Pete had gotten a haircut and had vowed to shave and shower every day.

Lucia liked to dress up and wear her bling on cruises. She especially liked the dress-up days on the ships, when she could wear her glitziest dresses and jewelry. She was an attractive lady at sixty-five. She had brown eyes, and her hair was black with streaks of gray. She had a nicely shaped nose and a friendly face with a ready smile for friends or strangers. She had a closet full of tasteful clothes. She loved jewelry, so Pete always made sure he got her jewelry on special occasions, like birthdays or anniversaries. Pete had surprised her with a fortieth anniversary gift of two-carat-diamond stud earrings. She was thrilled with the gift and planned to wear them on the cruise, along with other jewelry.

As they finished packing, Lucia referred to her checklist to make sure nothing was forgotten. The last thing on the list was medication. Lucia and Pete both had hypertension and high cholesterol, so it was important that they took their medication every day.

"Did you remember to bring your pills?" asked Lucia.

"I have them all in my pillbox," answered Pete.

Lucia saw a small pill container next to Pete's pillbox. She looked at the writing on the container. "You're bringing Viagra? How many are in there?"

"Seven."

"*Tu sei pazzo*! (You're crazy!)" yelled Lucia. "Do you want to give both of us heart attacks? We're not young bunnies anymore."

"But I want to celebrate our anniversary on the ship. Did you bring any K-Y Jelly?"

"Maybe." Lucia blushed.

Pete grinned and grabbed her buttocks. "Why don't we have a preview of coming attractions?"

Lucia slapped his hand away. "The Uber is coming in thirty minutes, you horny old goat. Let's finish packing."

Dave and Camille also lived in the southern part of Burlington, in a twelve-room colonial. They had three and one-half baths, four bedrooms, a finished basement, and an enclosed porch that had been converted into a year-round solarium. They had recently remodeled their en suite bathroom, taking out the tub. They had replaced it with a huge walk-in shower. There were other tubs in other bathrooms that Camille could soak in for hours and relax with a glass of champagne. In their driveway was Camille's car, a BMW X-3, and Dave's car, an Audi Q-5. Each car was equipped with all-wheel drive. The house and cars were fully paid for because Dave was involved in a serious automobile accident one year after college. While driving through an intersection, his car was T-boned by a small truck that had ran a red light. Luckily, Dave was wearing his seat belt, but he still suffered multiple broken bones. He'd sued the trucking company and was awarded a $2 million settlement. With the proceeds, he and Camille had bought their house and cars. The rest of the money had been invested in an eclectic variety of stocks, bonds, and bank deposits. Their portfolio had grown over the years, and their financial future was solid. It still took Dave months to recover from his broken bones and an additional year of physical therapy to walk normally. He exercised religiously to build up the muscles in his back, arms, and legs, but the remnants of the accident remained with him, especially on those frigid Vermont days. He welcomed the warm and soothing climes of Florida and the Caribbean.

Dave and Camille loved their lifestyle and their jobs. They were both thirty-five and had talked about having children, but as time went by, they were very happy with the status quo. They loved to lay back on cruise ships, dressed casually in shorts, T-shirts, and bathing suits. They loved to soak up the sun while reading and relaxing by the pool. But like Lucia, they also liked to dress up and show off their fancy wardrobes and jewelry. They were both beautiful people who liked to flaunt their affluence. They were happily anticipating this anniversary cruise. They had officially started the vacation in the early morning hours by making love in their new walk-in shower. As they finished packing, Camille referenced her checklist to make sure they were ready.

Phillip was excited about the technology that his friend had developed. He couldn't wait to get back on the ship and test it. His friend had developed a phone app that could access the combination to any safe. All you had to do was place the phone against the safe, and the combination would be displayed on the screen. Phillip was an honest person. He had never cheated anyone or committed any type of crime. He had never even gotten a parking ticket. He thought of what it would mean to have access to all the safes on the cruise. Everyone on the ship had a safe in their room, even the workers below deck. Patrons on the cruise, especially women, had thousands of dollars' worth of jewelry and other valuables. If he could somehow devise a plan to get into these safes, he would become a rich man.

As he pondered this scenario, he wondered if it was worth the risk. He thought of the poor pay and the poor living conditions on the ship. He thought of his future prospects if he left this job. There were not many opportunities for him at home. It might be worth the risk, so he should at least come up with a plan. If the plan looked feasible, he might put it into action. In order for his scam to be successful, he had to organize it to the minutest detail, enlisting a lot of people who he would have to pay off. He might be able to get enough willing participants, because many of his colleagues were also frustrated with the low pay and poor living arrangements. But first, he would have to orchestrate the many moving parts into a beautiful, successful symphony.

Phillip took out a piece of notebook paper and jotted down some questions and ideas. How could he get into someone's room in order to access to their safe? What would he take from the safe? He would only take small valuable items, like rings, earrings, and gold chains. If a person went into their safe for one of those items, they would think they had misplaced or lost it. They would not think someone had stolen it. When could he get access to the safe? Everyone's room was cleaned every day. Maybe he could enlist some of the porters who cleaned the room. He would need lookouts in the hallway to warn of any approaching patrons. If one of his people could get into the room, it would take them a minute to access the combination, open the safe, and take the jewelry.

How would he know what rooms had valuable jewelry? The waiters! He could have waiters at the buffet, restaurants, and casino act as lookouts. The waiters would see anyone wearing small, valuable jewelry. Whenever patrons ordered drinks, the waiters took their room cards to the cashier, who then credited the items to respective rooms. The waiter could indicate to the cashier that a patron was wearing a valuable item, and the cashier could write their room number on a separate piece of paper that they would give to Phillip. But how would the cashier know when to put a patron's room number on a separate piece of paper? Phillip thought of a signal that the waiter could give the cashier. The waiter would touch the side of their nose. That gesture would go unnoticed by everyone. How would Phillip sell all the jewelry? On port days, workers were allowed to leave the ship and sightsee. Phillip would have to canvas various jewelry stores and see if any of them would fence the jewelry. He was certain he would be able to find some dishonest proprietors to accept the contraband. He would insist on being paid in American dollars. There would be many people to pay off. His plan needed refinement, but he was confident that it would work.

When Phillip arrived at the *Acme* for his new assignment, he immediately went to his room below deck. Since this was a new room and a new ship for him, he had to assign himself a new combination for his safe. He assigned the numbers four, four, nine, seven as his new combination. He waited several minutes to see if the phone app worked. His heart pounded audibly in his chest, and beads of sweat appeared on his upper lip and brow as he waited. Finally, he decided to try it. He opened the app on his phone and placed it against the safe so that he could see the phone's screen. There was a beep, and the numbers four, four, nine, seven appeared on the screen.

His heart pounded even faster, and his breath came in short gasps as he looked at the screen in shocked excitement. The app worked! What would he do now? He had to think long and hard about his plan. He would have to take some people into his confidence. Luckily, his roommate from his last assignment, Donald Cruz, would also be his roommate on the *Acme*. Phillip decided to present his plan to Donald as a hypothetical possibility, not as a fait accompli. He wanted to get Donald's reaction to breaking the law first.

CHAPTER 3

Donald arrived the next morning. He and Phillip were busy most of the day with orientation and meetings. After dinner, they had time to relax, watch some television, and have a cocktail. They both decided to go back to their room and get some rest, because they had early assignments in the breakfast buffet the next morning. As they settled into their beds, Phillip thought he would get Donald's opinion of his plan.

"I know we've often discussed the poor living and working conditions and the low wages on the ship," Phillip started. "Suppose there was a way to make more money, but the plan was a bit dangerous. Would you be interested?"

"It would have to be a good plan and a lot of money," Donald said. "Like you, I'm totally frustrated. The salary is a pittance. I send most of it home to my family and am hardly left with anything to spend on myself. All we do is work—sometimes more than twelve hours. There's hardly any time for pleasure. I'm all ears."

"So, let me get this straight. You don't care if you get involved in a scam that could possibly lead to prison time if you get caught? I'm not going to tell you anything about my plan if you have any reservations."

"This job is like a prison but with better food. What's

your plan, and how much money are we talking about? I won't tell a soul."

"I can't give you a definitive amount for the money, but you could possibly double or triple your salary—or maybe even more. Remember, this is only a hypothetical plan. I'm not kidding. You can't tell anyone else about it. I want to get your opinion."

"Keep going," Donald said.

"You know how women like to wear their very expensive jewelry, especially during the dress-up days?" Phillip asked. "Their jewelry is worth thousands of dollars. Suppose there was a foolproof way of getting this jewelry?"

"Sounds like something that would be impossible."

"They keep all of their jewelry in their stateroom safes. Suppose there was a way of getting into those safes without being detected?"

"I can't think of any way that this would work. How the hell would you get their combinations? You'd have to bribe the porters who clean the rooms. So far, your plan isn't making any sense."

"Hear me out. When I was back home, a computer friend of mine developed a technology that would take care of that problem. It's an app that can access the combination to a safe. All you have to do is open the app, place the phone against the safe with the screen facing you, and the safe's combination will be displayed on the screen."

Donald's eyes lit up. "Does anyone else know about

this? I've never heard of it. What good does it do us if it's back home in Quezon, not here?"

"This app is totally new. Hardly anyone knows about it. Are you still serious about being part of this? Because I'm going to tell you something that only we can know. If I tell you the rest of my plan, you cannot—under any circumstances—tell anyone else without telling me first. If you do, there will be dire consequences. I'm not kidding. Should I continue?"

"This is getting serious, but I promise not to tell this secret to anyone. What is it?"

"I have the app on my phone," said Philip.

Donald stared at Philip incredulously. "I don't believe you. How can an app do what you say?"

"I'm going to prove it to you. I'll give you my phone. I want you to put the phone against your safe. I'll look away, so I don't see your combination."

Philip opened the app and handed his phone to Donald. Then he looked away as Donald placed the phone against his safe. The numbers nine, three, five, two appeared on the screen.

"Holy shit!" exclaimed Donald.

"My computer friend wanted me to test the app when I got back on the ship. He hasn't told anyone else about it. When I tried it on my safe, I was astonished—just like you. It makes my idea very feasible, but I'm going to need a lot of help. Do you know any people who might be interested?

I'm going to need more waiters and cashiers specifically, and they must be sworn to secrecy."

The Christoses enjoyed a pleasant flight to Fort Lauderdale. They spent the night at the Hilton and, the next day, were fast tracked to their room on the ship. Their suites were exquisite, and their balconies were wide and roomy with comfortable deck chairs and a large table where they could enjoy cocktails or feast their eyes on the shimmering turquoise Atlantic. They watched the waves crest toward the ship. Closer to the ship, the foaming, undulating waves were azure blue, but as they looked to the horizon, the waves turned to pewter and then to steel gray as they disappeared into the misty horizon. The clouds in the sky were dabs of cotton that sea gulls and pelicans flew between in a crisscross pattern. The Christoses could hear the waves as well as see them. The relaxing melody soothed their souls.

This was a new ship—only three months old—so everything in the suites was new, sparkly, and top notch. After their luggage was delivered, the two couples organized their toiletries, clothes, and medication. Their valuables were placed in the safe. The only thing they needed was the room card, which could be used to purchase anything: dinner, drinks, money at the casino, and gifts at the variety of shops on the ship. All they had to do was give their cards to the cashier, and the cashier would credit their room account. Patrons did not need to carry credit cards or wallets. Most patrons carried their room card on a lanyard draped around their necks.

There were many amenities provided to patrons with suites. One of those amenities was the availability of a butler. Eileen Acquino was assigned to the Christoses since they had adjoining suites. She was a native of Davao City, the third largest city in the Philippines. She was five feet six with brown eyes and wavy brown hair that was neatly combed back. She was wearing a neatly pressed white shirt, a dark tie, and dark slacks. Eileen was there to tend to their every need. She was very much like a mother hen and sometimes a drill sergeant. She introduced herself to Lucia and Pete after they finished unpacking, outlining her responsibilities in detail.

There was one detail that Pete did not want interfered with. He'd had trouble with a stiff neck for some time and had tried many different pillows, but they only seemed to exacerbate the problem. Nothing seemed to help his stiff neck, until he found an old pillow in his closet one day. He tried that pillow, and after a while, his neck was getting better. He soon found that if he placed a towel under the pillow, elevating it, his neck got even better. His stiff neck completely disappeared, so whenever Pete traveled anywhere, he took his favorite pillow and towel with him. When Eileen finished her spiel, Pete explained his special pillow and towel. He wanted to make sure the porters would not replace his pillow with ones from the cruise. Pete wanted to use his own pillow and towel every night. He didn't want it trifled with.

Eileen had never heard of such a thing. "You brought your own pillow and towel?" she asked. "We have pillows here that are very comfortable."

"I know you have pillows," said Pete, "but I want that pillow because it helps with my stiff neck."

"Are you sure? We have very comfortable pillows."

"I know you do, but I want *that* pillow and *that* towel on my bed when I go to sleep. I don't want anything else."

"OK, if that's what you want," said Eileen.

"She's *testa dura* (hardheaded)," Lucia whispered.

"I'll take care of your every need, even if it's a towel and a pillow that you brought from home," said Eileen. She looked around and tidied up anything she thought was out of place. Then she went to Dave and Camille's suite to terrorize them.

CHAPTER 4

The suite class had its own restaurant, the Ampulla, and its own sun deck on the seventeenth level. The Ampulla was not serving lunch since most patrons were still checking in, so the Christoses had lunch at the buffet on the fourteenth level. There you could select from many cuisines around the world. The women selected a table with an ocean view. The men sat down to save the table while the women grabbed their lunches. They came back with heaping trays of salad doused with ranch dressing, mussels in a wine-and-shallot sauce, and egg drop soup. As they settled into their seats, the men left to get one of their favorite dishes, rotini Bolognese, and small salads with Italian dressing. Everyone was extremely content with their lunch.

While they were eating, a very handsome waiter walked by and asked if they wanted anything to drink. The waiter was six feet three with black hair that was neatly coiffed. His eyes were blue, and his skin was deeply tanned. He wore a white shirt, blue tie, and charcoal slacks. He was extremely polite and cheerful. The ladies ordered sauvignon blanc, and the men ordered Heinekens. Even though it was early in the afternoon, the vacation had begun.

After taking the Christoses' orders, the waiter wandered, taking care of other patrons. Then, in a beautiful baritone voice, he started to sing, "Blue skies smiling at me. Nothing but blue skies do I see. Blue birds, where have they gone?"

The patrons in the buffet all clapped at the impromptu performance.

The waiter said, "I am Phillip. Have a wonderful day. If you want anything, just ask me." Then he left the buffet to get the Christoses' drinks.

When Phillip returned with their drinks, Lucia said, "That was beautiful, Phillip. You have such a lovely voice. Where are you from?"

"Thank you," said Phillip. "I'm from Quezon in the Philippines. I want to make sure everyone is happy while they're here. If you need anything, just ask me. I truly mean it."

After lunch, the Christoses took a leisurely tour of the ship. There were several spots they really wanted to check out. At the Retreat, tea, coffee, sandwiches, and pastries were served every day from three thirty to four thirty. One could also go there any time to relax and order wine, beer, or cocktails. If you had problems with the ship's Wi-Fi, someone was always there to help you. The Christoses also visited the casino, which was not yet open. The casino was never open while the ship was at port. It only opened when the ship was at sea, which would be that night. The casino had all their favorite slot machines, as well as roulette and card games. The cashier was at one end of the casino, and at the other end was the bar, the bartender, and a gigantic seventy-inch smart TV. They could each enjoy their favorite cocktail while watching sporting matches. Waiters and porters roamed the casino, helping patrons with their questions or problems.

The Christoses would return to the casino after the show and dinner tonight. The shows provided entertainment from all genres because the cruise director had attempted to appeal to all tastes. A comedian was scheduled for tonight. Other performances included concert pianists, magicians, Broadway-themed extravaganzas, and singers. The cruise's talented orchestra backed up each performance. The performances were eclectic and entertaining.

There were also all sorts of activities at all times. Excursions were planned for every port. Every day, there were lectures on a variety of topics, art shows, dance classes, bingo, and trivia games. Lucia and Camille loved the trivia games. They often dragged their husbands along for their help with sport questions. Pete was especially knowledgeable about fifties and sixties rock and roll, and Dave took care of seventies and eighties music. The family often won the main prize, a ballpoint pen with the cruise's name embossed on the side.

On the seventeenth level, a sun deck was available for suite patrons. This was popular with the sunbathers, who would languish on the deck's reclining chairs all day to get some rays. Patrons would go there early in the morning to reserve a deck chair. One of the more popular chairs was called a clamshell. It was a round rattan chair, approximately five feet in diameter, and it was hooded with a white canvas that protected its user from the sun. A small cafe on that deck provided the sunbathers with a light lunch of hamburgers, wraps, and salads. The deck orderlies would provide towels, take drink orders, and deliver lunch to the person's deck chair. Suite patrons could get a tan while enjoying the ocean breeze and viewing fishing boats, yachts, or other cruise ships. They could also enjoying their favorite cocktail, wine or beer. It was incredibly relaxing. All the Christoses liked to use the deck for part of the day. When they got back to the snow in Burlington, Vermont, they would show off their tans to jealous friends and colleagues. Lucia and Camille enjoyed taking a dip in the pool. Pete and Dave liked to surf the internet and sport sites. They also liked to ogle pretty, young women when their wives weren't watching.

Dave and Camille expected to have a wonderful time on the cruise. There were some things they were interested in that Lucia and Pete were not. They wanted to check out all of the excursions. They planned to do as many as possible since they had never been to most of the islands on the itinerary. They also loved to dance, so they were interested in ballroom dancing. They noticed that there were dance classes offered where they could brush up on all the latest crazes, as well as be schooled in the lindy hop, the fox trot, the East and West Coast swings, and the Viennese waltz. Even though they loved the casino and expected to spend a lot of time there, they planned to leave it early most nights so that they could go to the King's Room Ballroom. There, they would drink cocktails and dance to the band and disc jockeys. They would twist, twirl, dip, and wobble into the wee hours of the night. Then they would go back to their stateroom, have sex, and fall into an exhausted sleep.

CHAPTER 5

Phillip's plan had reached the point where he was ready to test it. Donald Cruz was the perfect accomplice. He was a butler, and butlers had access to their patrons' rooms at any time. They could get into the room, access the safe's combination, open it, and take the contraband. All the butlers knew each other. They had a supervisor and weekly meetings that coincided with the start of each new cruise. The butlers' new assignments were posted during these meetings. Butlers were only assigned to patrons in the suite class, and they were each responsible for twelve suites. Suites started at $7,000 dollars and could range as high as $45,000, depending on the size of the suite and the amenities provided. Patrons who rented suites were very affluent.

The casino was the perfect place to identify anyone wearing expensive jewelry, and luckily, Phillip was assigned to the casino. He'd recruited the bartender for his scheme. On the first night, the casino was packed. Patrons mingled and talked among the cacophony of ringing and clanging machines and screeching craps and roulette players celebrating their winnings. Phillip kept busy, showing patrons how to access their room accounts to use as gambling money. He noticed Hilda Burrows, a woman with a big, gaudy, sparkling diamond ring. He estimated that it was more than five carats and worth thousands of dollars.

After Phillip showed Hilda how to access her room account, she asked if he could get her a vodka martini with a twist, giving him her room card. Phillip told the bartender to make a vodka martini with a twist, handed him the room card, and then gave him the special signal, placing his finger on the side of his nose. When the bartender saw the special signal, he wrote the room number on a separate piece of paper. Phillip returned with Hilda's vodka martini. She flashed her ring as she pushed the buttons on the slot machine. Then she asked him several more questions about accessing her room account. She wanted to make sure she had enough money to play for the rest of the evening.

Eventually Phillip moved on to help other people. He noticed many women wearing expensive jewelry, like diamond rings, diamond earrings, diamond and gold bracelets, and pearl necklaces. He felt like a prospector at Sutter's Mill during the gold rush of 1849, but he didn't have to pan for gold. It was right there for the taking. Although there were many prospective marks, Phillip decided to concentrate on one person to see if his plan could be completed successfully. He would have to do some research and employ the butler who was assigned to Hilda's room. Donald could tell Phillip who was assigned to her room; he had the list of butler assignments.

The next day, Donald checked the room assignment for Hilda and John Burrows. The butler assigned to their room was Eileen Acquino, a fellow Filipino. Donald knew Eileen. She was headstrong, opinionated, and a control freak. He feared approaching her with the scheme. He would have to do a convincing sales job and threaten her with bodily harm if she divulged the plan to anyone.

He approached her below deck during one of their daily breaks and asked, "Eileen, may I speak with you for a minute?"

"Sure, Donald, but make it snappy. My break is almost over," said Eileen.

"Are you interested in making some extra money? Probably a lot of extra money."

"Are you suggesting a part time job? I'm already busting my hump working ten- and twelve-hour shifts."

"This would not involve any extra time. It would be an opportunity for a windfall."

"Everybody is interested in making more money. The pay here is horrendous. What is it?"

"What I'm going to tell you, you cannot ever tell anyone else," Donald warned. "If anyone else knows about this plan, we'll know it was you. We haven't told anyone else. You're the first. You'll be risking bodily harm if you tell anyone else. Should I go on?"

Eileen questioningly stared at Donald for several long seconds. "How much money are we talking about?"

"You could double or triple your salary. You might make even more than that. Butlers are integral to the plan."

"Is it against the law? If I get caught, could I go to jail?"

"Yes, but if the plan is executed correctly, no one, except the participants, will know."

Eileen stared at Donald for several more seconds. She thought about more than tripling her salary. She had no husband or family, but she wanted to build up a nest egg for her retirement. Eventually, she said, "Tell me about it."

"Remember, you are risking bodily harm if you tell anyone. Are you sure you want to know?"

"I'm sure."

With rapt, wide-eyed astonishment, Eileen listened to Donald explain the plan in detail. It seemed foolproof. She was excited with the prospect of tripling her salary.

"This will be our initial run," Donald continued explaining. "I think Hilda only wears that expensive ring at night, but that's something that you will have to check. Make sure she's not wearing the ring. Then, using the phone app, open her safe and take the ring. She was drunk last night. She'll think she lost it. I know you're a meticulous person. The next time I see you, you'll have the ring."

"You're right. I am meticulous, and I plan everything down to the smallest detail. The next time I see you, I will hand you the ring. I'm in! Here's to your plan." Eileen stuck her hand out and shook Donald's.

Later that day, Eileen was on the tenth floor, attending to some of her clients. Donald had given her the phone with the app. As she walked down the hall, she encountered Hilda and John Burrows. She checked out Hilda's hands. She was not wearing the ring.

"Hi, Hilda," Eileen said. "I hope you and John are having a great day."

"Hi, Eileen," said Hilda. "We're having a fantastic day. We're going up to the buffet to have lunch."

"Enjoy your lunch. Can I get you anything?"

"I can't think of anything. Thank you," said Hilda.

Eileen tended to another client before she went into John and Hilda's room. She stopped in front of the safe and placed the phone against it. To her shock and amazement, the combination appeared on the phone's screen. She opened the safe and saw the gaudy, multifaceted diamond ring on top of the couple's passports. She took the ring and closed the safe. Then she opened the door to the room and looked down the hallway. She wanted to make sure no one saw her leave the room. As she walked down the hall, all she could think about were dollar signs.

So far, the cruise was proving to be one of the best ever. It was relaxing, and the food was superb. The Christoses had even developed a tan that would be the envy of all Vermonters. Tonight was one of the dress-up nights. Lucia and Camille planned to wear their glitziest outfits, and

Lucia was going to wear the diamond earrings that Pete gave her. Maybe they would even celebrate their anniversary with a little nooky after they came back from the casino. Lucia would make sure Pete took Viagra, so he would be ready later.

The casino was hopping. It was a jeweler's paradise, as most of the women were bedecked in diamonds, pearls, gold, silver, rubies, and other jewels. Any type of jewelry that one could imagine was on display. Phillip worked hard, helping patrons with their questions and delivering their drinks. He'd indicated ten women who were wearing expensive jewelry to the cashier, and the cashier had written their room numbers on the special sheet. After Phillip had received Hilda Burrows's diamond ring from Eileen, he knew his plan worked. Eileen was intelligent and careful. She was a welcome addition to their little cabal.

Lucia was playing her favorite Cleopatra slot machine when she saw Phillip. She had already won one hundred dollars, while Pete, who was playing next to her, had lost fifty dollars. "Hi, Phillip. Would you be so kind as to bring me a vodka gimlet?" she asked.

"You could bring me a Manhattan straight up," said Pete.

"I'd be happy to," said Phillip as he eyed her expensive earrings. As he walk to the cashier, he knew Lucia would become one of his potential victims.

After spending time at the casino, Lucia and Pete returned to their rooms. Their butler, Eileen, had left a bottle of champagne as an anniversary gift. Pete popped the cork and poured the bubbly liquid into two long-stemmed champagne glasses. They sipped leisurely as they discussed the night's events. Lucia had won $200, while Pete had made a comeback. After being down one hundred dollars on the slot machines, he switched to roulette and blackjack, coming out ahead by $150.

They were both giddy as they finished their champagne and undressed each other. They threw the covers off the bed and made love. After all those years, they were still crazy about each other. After making love, they fell into a relaxed and contented sleep.

After work, Phillip decided to have a meeting with his coconspirators below deck, in Phillip's room. Phillip, Donald, and Eileen were in attendance, along with the bartender/cashier from the casino, James Mendoza, who was also Filipino. He was from Manila and had been working on various cruises for fifteen years. James was of medium height and stocky, weighing in at 210 pounds. He was slightly tanned with freckles. He had brown eyes and thinning brown hair that was graying at the temples. Phillip had known James for a number of years and knew he could be trusted.

"I want to thank you all for the great job you're all

doing," Phillip said. "Eileen gave me the diamond ring, which is worth thousands of dollars, and we got fifteen more possibilities in the casino tonight. Tomorrow we dock in St. Thomas. I'm going to get off the ship and see if I can find a jeweler who will fence the ring. The jeweler will need to have outlets all over the Virgin Islands."

"Are we going into any other rooms?" asked Donald.

"I want Eileen to look at our list of rooms to see if she services any of them," Phillip said. "Donald, I'd also like you to look at the list. If there are any rooms that neither of you service, see who the butler is. This is critical. I want both of you to determine whether or not we can trust any of the other butlers. If we can't trust them, we won't go into any of those rooms. It's too risky. We want to keep what we're doing tight—just us if possible. I don't want to involve many other people. I think we can make enough money with just the four of us. We'll meet again tomorrow night, and I'll report if I've found a fence for our jewelry. Eileen and Donald will report on the other butlers. Wish me luck tomorrow, while I look for a dishonest jeweler.

CHAPTER 6

The next day, the ship docked at Charlotte Amalie in St. Thomas. Founded in 1666 by the Danes, the quaint island city was known for Thomas Synagogue, the second oldest synagogue in the United States. It was also known for its long history with pirates—particularly Bluebeard, whose castle was a US historical landmark. Colonial warehouse buildings had been converted into stores and urban malls.

Phillip disembarked from the ship and walked the narrow streets, looking for jewelers. After going into several legitimate jewelry stores, he came upon Carib Jewelers in one of the malls. He entered the store and was immediately energized by the refreshing air conditioning. He walked up and down the long aisles, looking into the large rectangular jewelry cases.

Eventually, a salesperson walked over and asked, "May I help you find something? We have great discounts."

"I'm looking to sell rather than buy," said Phillip.

"Why don't I get the manager?"

The salesperson walked away, and a moment later, the manager appeared from his inner office. His name tag read Rama Shiva, manager.

"I understand you have some jewelry that you'd like to sell," said Rama. "Do you have this item with you?"

Phillip had wrapped the ring in a cloth, which he pulled out of his pocket. As he unwrapped it, Rama's eyes widened. "How much can you give me for this ring?"

Rama took the ring and examined it carefully with his loupe, turning it over so that he could examine each side. "I'll give you ten thousand dollars."

"Is that the best you can do? I'm going to have many more items to sell." Phillip winked imperceptibly.

"Understood," said Rama, examining the ring more carefully. "I'll give you twelve thousand dollars, but that's the highest I can go."

"Accepted. Can you pay me now, in cash—in American dollars?"

"Yes, I can."

"Do you have affiliates on other islands?"

"We have stores on all the islands," said Rama. "If you want to sell other items, mention my name. I'm the owner of all the stores. You won't have any trouble selling anything, as long as the quality is high. I'll go get your money."

After a moment, Rama returned with a large envelope filled with one-hundred-dollar bills. Phillip used Rama's office to count the money. He was extremely elated as he left Carib Jewelers and returned to the ship.

After rising early and having breakfast, Lucia and Pete boarded the bus for their St. Thomas excursion. Their itinerary included the Thomas Synagogue; a tour of

Bluebeard's Castle; and a bus ride up the green hills and mountains of St. Thomas, where they would stop for lunch and enjoy some callaloo soup and conch fritters.

They were boarding their bus after completing the tour of Bluebeard's Castle when Lucia saw Phillip walking by. She called to him to get his attention. "Phillip! Phillip, over here. Are you enjoying your time off the ship?"

"It's just wonderful to have some free time to enjoy the islands, even if it's only for a couple of hours," Phillip said.

"We'll probably see you in the casino again tonight," said Lucia. She and Pete smiled and waved as Phillip walked away.

Phillip noticed that Lucia was not wearing her earrings.

After returning from the excursion, Pete went to deck fifteen, where there was a special area for smokers. It was his favorite spot to hang out on the ship. There were comfortable chairs that overlooked the ocean. Pete sat on one. Then he took out his pipe, filled it to the brim with his apple-scented tobacco, and lit it. As he inhaled the fragrant tobacco smoke, he watched fishing boats float and seagulls dive bomb the deck, looking for crumbs. Pete was very content and relaxed, but he couldn't help overhearing the woman sitting adjacent to him.

"I don't know what happened to my diamond ring. I wore it to dinner and the show two nights ago, but now I can't find it. It's a gorgeous five-carat ring that my husband gave me on our thirtieth anniversary. I'm devastated about it."

Pete's detective ears perked up. "Do you mind if I ask you several questions?" He leisurely puffed and inhaled the pipe smoke before continuing. "My name is Pete Christos, and I'm a private investigator."

"No, I don't mind at all. My name is Hilda Burrows."

"Pleased to meet you, Hilda. Did you ever take the ring off? Maybe you took it off in the bathroom when you washed your hands. Can you think of any time at all when you might have taken it off?"

"Well, as I said, I wore it to dinner and a show. Then my husband and I went to the casino. We had quite a bit to drink that night, but I'm pretty sure I didn't take it off until we got back to the room, where I put it in the safe. But when I looked in the safe this morning, the ring wasn't there. I don't know if I misplaced it or dropped it somewhere. I'm so sick that I almost want to vomit. That ring is worth at least twenty thousand dollars. I had the porters who clean my room look for it in every possible nook and cranny, but they found nothing."

"Are you sure you didn't take the ring off for any reason?" asked Pete.

"No, I'm sure I kept it on my finger the whole time."

"The only thing that I can suggest is that you check the lost and found. I think it's on the third deck. Maybe some honest person found it and turned it in."

"That's a great idea, Pete. I'm going to run down there right after I finish my Marlboro. I feel better already."

Pete finished his pipe and then went to join his wife at the pool. It was time for fifties rock and roll trivia—Pete's specialty.

After work that night, Phillip met with his team to distribute the money. He had received $12,000 for the ring and would give each person their equal share. The team members were ecstatic when they received $3,000 each.

"This was just from one ring?" Eileen asked. "This is more than I make in a month. I can't believe it."

"I found a fence for the jewelry—Carib Jewelers," Phillip said. "They have stores all over the Virgin Islands. I met with the owner, Rama Shiva, and he said he would accept our jewelry as long as it was high quality. We can go to any of his outlets and get cash. We'll each continue to get an equal share. If we don't screw things up, we stand to make a lot of money."

"What do we do next?" asked Donald.

Phillip asked, "James, do you have the list of rooms with you? Let's take a look at the room numbers to see which ones are assigned to Donald and Eileen. If possible, we can hit those rooms tomorrow and get the ball rolling."

They examined the list of rooms. Donald was assigned to three of the rooms, and Eileen was assigned to four.

Phillip looked at Donald and Eileen. "Be smart. Make

sure the patrons are not wearing their jewelry and no one sees you going in or out of their rooms. There's no hurry. Let's be certain we're doing the job right. We can't take any chances. We can't make any mistakes. The app is only on my phone, so you two will have to share it and coordinate your hits. Work together. Communicate with each other, and keep me in the loop, because I have the phone. When you are done with your hit, give me the phone and the stolen jewelry. I will give the phone to the other person. Everything is working very smoothly so far, so let's keep it that way. We'll meet again tomorrow night. Oh, and another thing that's very important—don't let anyone see all this money. Hide it!"

The following day, Donald and Eileen decided on two possible hits each. Donald would have the phone in the morning. Then he would return it to Phillip, along with any stolen jewelry. Phillip would give the phone to Eileen for her afternoon jobs. Donald did not have any luck with his first attempt, since someone always seemed to be in the room. Either someone was cleaning the room, or the patrons had returned to use the bathroom. However, he was successful with his other hit. He was able to get into their safe and escape with another valuable diamond ring.

Eileen had more luck with Lucia and Pete Christos. They had gotten into a routine that never varied. They would have breakfast with Dave and Camille at 9:00 a.m. Then they would come back to the room to use the facilities before going to trivia. Afterward, they would go up to the private sun deck and stay until teatime in the Retreat at 3:30 p.m. That meant they would be out of the room all afternoon.

Eileen easily managed to enter the Christoses' safe and locate a light-blue rectangular box. When she opened the box, the earrings were inside, on top of some cotton. She took the earrings but left the cotton and the box in the safe. If Lucia looked for her earrings, she would think she had lost or misplaced them.

Eileen was also successful later in the afternoon, when she took another set of diamond earrings. She was two for two. Those two sets of diamond earrings could easily be worth $30,000. She knew Donald had also been successful. It turned out to be a very good day.

CHAPTER 7

"What do you mean you can't find your earrings?" Pete asked, as he got ready for the show and dinner.

"When I took them off at night, I put them in the blue box in the safe," Lucia said. "I want to wear them again tonight, but they're not in the box."

"I've seen you take them off and put them on the counter. You have to be more careful. I hope you didn't lose them." Pete's voice was getting louder with each sentence.

"Please don't raise your voice at me. This is very upsetting," said Lucia with tears in her eyes.

"I'm sorry, honey. Let's look around for them. Call Camille and Dave. They'll help us."

Lucia called next door. When Camille and Dave arrived, all four went over the room with a fine-tooth comb, but they couldn't find any trace of the earrings. Camille and Dave went to the early show, but Pete and Lucia went to the lost and found on the third deck. There was a short line forming behind them as Pete and Lucia inquired about her earrings.

"Sorry, Mrs. Christos, but no one has found your earrings. If they turn up, we will contact you immediately. It's funny, though. We've had several people inquire about lost jewelry in the last several days. It's very unusual."

Pete looked at Lucia. "Let's join Camille and Dave at the

show. We'll discuss what happened over dinner. I've been with you every day, and I can't imagine how or where you could have lost your earrings. I know you had them in the casino. Maybe you took them off in the bathroom, and they dropped on the floor. If so, the cleaners might have swept them up when they came. We'll figure it out, honey."

After the show, the Christoses went to the Luminaire for dinner. Lucia was extremely upset and could barely look at the menu. Pete was also upset, but he was hungry. He selected the crab cake appetizer and the rack of lamb. All four settled on the same thing.

As they sipped their wine and sampled their appetizers, Dave started the conversation. "Let's try to be analytical. Where were you and what were you doing the last time you were wearing your earrings?"

"What I remember," said Lucia, "is coming back from the casino. Eileen had left some champagne in the room because it was our anniversary. Pete popped the cork, and we both had two glasses. Then we—"

"You what?" asked Dave.

Lucia slightly blushed. "Then we celebrated our anniversary."

"There it is! That's it," said Dave. "You rolled around on the sheets. The earrings must have come off and fell on the floor. Then they were vacuumed up by the orderlies the next day."

"That's possible," said Pete. "We were rolling around on and under the covers a lot."

Lucia smacked Pete's arm.

"Listen, let's keep inquiring about the earrings the next time we see Eileen," said Pete. "I insured the earrings, and I'll put in a claim. They had a high deductible, but I'm sure I'll get a decent amount back. Then I'll buy you another pair of earrings. Let's enjoy the rest of the cruise. It's been wonderful, and I don't want to spoil it."

They all agreed with Pete's sentiment as they looked at the dessert menu.

St. Croix was the next stop on the ship's itinerary. Phillip had received the diamond ring and two pairs of diamond earrings from Eileen and Donald. He was going to find Carib Jewelers in St. Croix and cash in the jewelry. He was hoping to clear $40,000 after some negotiations. Many patrons had scheduled excursions and tours in St. Croix, so it would be easy for Eileen and Donald to enter those rooms and extract the contraband. Phillip had assigned them four rooms each.

While Donald was successfully getting into all four safes, he marveled at the ease of it. He was starting to feel somewhat greedy and selfish. If he and Eileen were taking all the risks, why couldn't they get a few extra benefits? He should reap some extra rewards for all his efforts. If he said there was no jewelry in the safe, how would they know he was lying? They wouldn't! There was no way of checking. He would give most of the jewelry to Phillip, but he would keep some for himself to cash later. Some of these items were worth $20,000 or more.

Donald felt justified in what he was thinking, but he had to be very careful not to get caught. It wasn't the authorities that he was concerned about. It was Phillip. Phillip had warned him about the dire consequences that would occur if anyone strayed, and he believed Phillip was serious about doling out bodily harm. Phillip was generally affable, but he was a big, strong man. When he was angry, he was scary.

At the meeting that evening, Phillip doled out $10,000 to each team member. To their delight, the money was piling up, and there were no indications that anyone thought what was happening was anything but misplaced or lost jewelry. No one seemed to think there was a conspiracy, so Phillip gave Donald and Eileen the green light for more assignments. They saw no reason to hold back or slow down.

The next day was a sea day, so everyone would be aboard the ship, making it more difficult to enter the rooms. Phillip told Eileen and Donald to try to get into the rooms tomorrow, but there was no hurry. It would be easier to get into the rooms when the ship docked at its next stop, Cozumel, Mexico. This was a popular spot since people wanted to see the Mayan ruins at Tulum and Chichén Itzá. Many people would disembark and take excursions. Phillip planned to disembark and cash in more jewelry.

Lucia and Pete were students of the Mayan civilization. They had read extensively about it and were highly anticipating their excursion in Cozumel. They planned to see the ruins in Tulum and the pyramids in Chichén Itzá. On a previous vacation, they had toured Tikal National Park in Guatemala. This grand metropolis once held over sixty thousand people, but it had been mysteriously abandoned in the tenth century. New facts and discoveries were constantly being unearthed. A new laser mapping system called Lidar was able to locate structures that were normally hidden in the jungle by using light waves to create three-dimensional maps. It had been used to discover superhighways and structures.

Lucia and Pete also loved Mexican food. They loved to sample local cuisines. Lunch was included on their excursion, so they stopped at an open-air restaurant in Cozumel. There, they sampled *panuchos*, which were famous throughout the Mayan Peninsula. They were fried tortillas filled with refried beans, shredded chicken, purple onions, avocado, tomato sauce, and lettuce. They were delicious.

That evening, they were invited to attend a meet and greet with the ship's captain, Karin Klein, and her staff. That was to be followed by dinner at the captain's table in the captain's special dining quarters. This area was reserved for the captain and her crew. Only a few people were invited to dine there. Lucia and Pete received an invite because Lucia had known Captain Klein for a number of years, since Lucia was one of the top-selling travel agents. She had steered hundreds of customers to Sea Atlantic cruises. Lucia and Pete had attended previous dinners at the captain's table and didn't want to miss the elegant dinner.

Captain Klein was forty-eight years old and five feet seven. She had hazel eyes, short brown hair that she wore in a side-swept style, and a perfectly shaped nose. Her kind face always displayed the hint of a smile, and she loved to wear Christian Louboutin heals that added several inches to her height. She wore a white shirt and a dark tie. Her navy blue suit was festooned with epaulets and four stripes. She looked accessible, and she was as beautiful as she was intelligent. Captain Klein had the highest rank on the ship. She had become enamored with cruising at a young age. When she was twelve, her parents had taken her on a cruise to South America. From that initial trip, she knew she wanted to be involved with cruises for the rest of her life. She attended college and the Maritime Academy, working her way up from menial jobs on a variety of ships. Eight years ago, she reached the pinnacle—captain of the *Acme*.

Captain Klein's second in command was Nicholas Papas, a staff captain from Athens. Her third in command was a hotel director from San Francisco, Ryan Simpson. Boris Boyko, a chief engineer from Kyiv, was fourth in command, and he was in charge of all things mechanical.

The dinner was elegance personified. The waiters were all dressed in tuxedos. The tableware was silver and gold. The dishes and cups were exquisite china. The menu included a crab stack with corn custard and passion caviar; sirloin that was aged for thirty-six days and served with an almond and potato puree; pan-grilled duck with elderberry cider, onions, and a dark-cherry glaze; and veal with crushed green apples and a light cheese broth. The champagne flowed constantly.

Lucia loved to talk to Captain Klein about the ship and its new technology. Even though they appeared unwieldy, these sleek vessels could streak forward at thirty knots, back up, and go sideways when they parked next to other cruise ships. They were truly agile marvels. It was mind boggling that Captain Klein could efficiently orchestrate all the parts for a smooth and successful cruise. While Lucia talked to Captain Klein, Pete talked to Boris about all the mechanical aspects of the ship.

After the elegant dinner, Captain Klein took Pete and Lucia aside and said, "I'd like to know if you could do me a favor. I have a problem that I hope you will help me with. There are an unusual number of patrons—all women— who seem to have misplaced their jewelry. They have made inquiries at the lost and found. Pete, I know you and Dave are detectives. I'd like you to do a little investigating. Is this just a coincidence, or is something more serious happening? If it is something more serious, it's bad publicity and bad for business. I'd have to bring in the FBI. I'd like to avoid that and handle it in house if possible."

"Did you know I lost my diamond earrings?" asked

Lucia. "They were an anniversary gift from Pete. I'm very upset by their disappearance."

"I'm so sorry to hear that," said Captain Klein. "Unfortunately, I've heard that scenario a lot. It's becoming a common occurrence. If someone is behind this, we have to stop them and fast! I would appreciate you doing inquiries, Pete. You will have full cooperation from our security team and anyone else you think could be helpful."

"I will gladly help you," said Pete.

"If you find anything, report it directly to me," said Captain Klein. "And to show my appreciation, I'm going to comp any of our specialty restaurants that you and your guests choose to eat at for the rest of the cruise."

"That's very generous of you, Karin," said Pete. "Dave and I will start immediately."

CHAPTER 8

"Dave, we've got a job," said Pete.

"Good," said Dave. "You mean when we get home?"

"No, now."

"Dad, we're on vacation. What do you mean now?"

"Karin Klein wants us to investigate a rash of lost jewelry. She thinks there might be more to it than just people getting careless. She's going to comp our meals at any of the specialty restaurants for our efforts."

"That's nice of her, but I thought we agreed that Mom accidentally lost her jewelry. This is going to spoil the vacation."

"I don't think so," said Pete. "We can still do what we've been doing every day. We can go on our excursions, but we should keep our eyes and ears open, looking for patterns. Besides, we've been asked by the captain. She wants to keep the FBI out of it for now. If they come on board and start sniffing around, it'll be bad publicity. Captain Klein wants to keep the status quo by investigating this in house. If we find something tangible, she'll call in the authorities. She has confidence that we will find something. More women than usual are losing their expensive jewelry. They can't all be that careless. I remember talking to a lady in the area where I smoke my pipe. I think her name was Hilda. She described losing her ring in exactly the same fashion that your mom lost her earrings. She remembers putting it in the safe, but it wasn't there the next day."

"I don't think anyone can get into the safes after the combinations are set. I would think anyone who has access to the room safes is highly supervised."

"That's something that we'll have to check out. Why don't we give Eileen a call and ask if she has seen anything suspicious? We'll tell her that we're still trying to find your mother's earrings. Do you have her card?"

Eileen happened to be in the area, tending to other guests, when Pete and Dave called her. She was able to come to their room quickly. As she entered, she saw them both sitting on the sofa. She had to remind herself to appear calm, but it was intimidating, seeing them both sit there.

"What's up, guys?" she asked. "Is anything wrong? Did I forget to deliver your afternoon wine and fruit? What can I do for you?"

"We're still searching for Lucia's earrings," said Pete. "We haven't given up. We're trying to trace exactly what happened and wondered if you could shed any light on it. She said she put them in her blue box in the safe. Did you hear anything from the orderlies who cleaned the room? Did they find anything or hear anything loud when they were vacuuming?"

"I'm surprised you haven't given up on this," said Eileen. "I haven't heard anything from the orderlies or anyone else.

I come in every day, and everything seems normal. Nothing seems to be out of place."

"If you see anything out of the ordinary or hear of anyone finding anything, please let us know," said Dave. "Those earrings were very expensive."

"I will certainly let you know," said Eileen. Then she left the room.

Shortly after, the men left to meet their wives for cappuccinos and pastries at the coffee bar. After finishing their pastries and cappuccinos, Pete suggested that he and Dave visit the lost and found staff, who were part of the purser department, and the housekeeping staff. Both were stationed on the third level. Once there, Pete and Dave introduced themselves to the lost and found staff, but before they could continue, the purser interrupted them.

"We know who you are and why you're here. Captain Klein had a meeting with the staff. She urged us to give you our full cooperation. Everything we say to you and everything you do will be held in the strictest of confidence. How can I help?"

"Could you please give me the names and room numbers of all the people who have lost jewelry?" asked Pete. "Also, could you give me a list of people who have access to those rooms—porters, butlers, and anyone else?"

"As soon as we amass this information, we'll leave a message on your phone, and you can pick it up at your convenience," said the purser. "Is there anything else I can help you with?"

"Is there any way that a person could get into someone else's safe?" asked Pete

"There are people who can help patrons reset their combinations. Some people forget their combinations or punch in the wrong numbers and press enter. This messes up the original combination, which will not work anymore. It has to be reset with a new combination. There are people from this office who can help with that; however, someone who doesn't know the combination cannot get into the safe. It's impossible. Only the programmers with access to a master code can do it. But these programmers are constantly monitored and highly regulated by the purser staff."

"So a person couldn't get into a safe unless they knew the combination or were a programmer with the master code," Dave reiterated.

"That's right. It has never been done. If a person could breach someone else's safe, it would be devastating to the ship's security. That's why the rules are so stringent."

"Thank you," said Pete. "We appreciate your help." He and Dave left to go up to the Sun Deck.

As they were entering the elevator, Dave said, "You know, the more we investigate this, the more frustrating it becomes. The only plausible explanation seems to be that someone is getting into the safes and stealing the jewelry, but according to the purser, that's impossible. It reminds me of that old detective story by Edgar Allen Poe, 'Murders in the Rue Morgue.' A murder is committed in a locked room, where no one could get in or out. Do you remember that one, Dad?"

"It's one of my favorites," said Pete. "In the end, Inspector Dupin figured it out. We have two brains working, so if this was a crime, we'll figure it out too."

Phillip returned from Carib Jewelers in Cozumel with $60,000. It was the biggest haul yet, with each of the four receiving $15,000. They had so many one-hundred-dollar bills that they were running out of places to hide them. There were too many to put in their safes, so they put the money in their luggage, which they kept under their beds.

"I had an encounter today that might be a problem," said Eileen. "I'd like to get your opinions." She had the attention of Phillip, Donald, and James.

"Go on," said Phillip.

"I got a call from Pete and Dave Christos, asking me to go to Pete's room. I was a little intimidated when I got there. They were both sitting on the sofa and glaring at me."

"What did they want?" asked Donald.

"They asked me more questions about Lucia's missing jewelry. They haven't given up on looking for her lost earrings because they were so expensive. They wanted to know if I had found or seen anything suspicious. Do you think we have anything to worry about? It's not good if two detectives start snooping around."

"I don't think we have anything to worry about," said Phillip. "They're looking for a needle in a haystack. They're not going to find anything."

"I mentioned that they're both detective, didn't I? They're looking for clues, and if they keep digging, they might find something. I'm getting a little concerned."

"Don't get rattled," said Phillip. "Keep your cool. If they question you again, tell them you don't know anything. Be calm. Guys like that can sense when you're not being straight with them. If they become a problem, I'll put some spoiled milk in Pete's cappuccino. That'll put him out of commission for a couple of days. By then, the cruise will be over, and he'll be out of our hair. Don't worry."

"Do you think we should scale back a little bit, until the cruise is over?" asked James.

"I don't think so," said Phillip. "There's so much expensive jewelry on this ship. It's a bonanza. I think we should continue to take advantage of the situation, since things are going so smoothly. There's too much money to be made. Our next port is Aruba, and I expect to cash in more jewelry there."

"When will it be enough money for you, Phillip?" asked Eileen.

"It'll never be enough," Phillip said, raising his voice. "I hope you're not getting cold feet, Eileen. I hope you're not going to mess it up for us. Remember what I told you in the beginning. We're in too deep now. I'm not afraid of throwing someone overboard in the dead of night. I don't care if you're a woman." Phillip's face had turned red.

"Calm down!" Eileen yelled. "I'm not going to mess anything up. I'm just voicing some concerns, and I really don't appreciate you threatening me. I'm not afraid of you. You're nothing but a big, no-good, goddamn bully. Just try something with me and see what happens."

The situation was getting tense. Thinking he should defuse the fireworks, James said, "I have some scotch in my room. Let's all cool off, relax, and have a drink. Then we can decide where we're all going to hide all this money."

CHAPTER 9

At the next port, the Christoses planned to go to Eagle Beach. The beaches in Aruba were pristine, and the ocean was turquoise and calm. They wanted to spend a relaxing day on the beach, making their bodies even more bronze in the baking sun. But before they left the boat, Pete and Dave went to the purser to get the information that they had requested. It had been neatly typed and placed in a large envelope. They wanted to look at it while sunbathing on the beach.

After the Christoses disembarked from the ship, they took a taxi to Eagle Beach. They had all their beach gear with them and were able to rent chairs and beach umbrellas. They found a spot close to Mama's Food Truck, which was parked at the beach for the day. The truck offered Aruban steak, pork chops, and chicken. Each meal came with a side of rice, plantains, or fries The Christoses smelled wonderful aromas as beach patrons lined up for lunch.

After they all settled, they took a dip in the ocean. Then they came back to their spot, lathered themselves in suntan lotion, and relaxed in the baking sun. Pete had brought his pipe. He moved slightly away from everyone, so the smoke wouldn't bother them. As he inhaled the fragrant pipe smoke, he looked at the information provided by the purser. He was startled to see that half the women who lost their jewelry were serviced by Eileen Acquino, their butler. The other women were serviced by Donald Cruz.

Pete called Dave over. "You won't believe this, Dave. Half the women who lost jewelry have the same butler— Eileen Acquino."

"You know, I thought Eileen looked nervous when we questioned her. Her eyes were darting all around the room. I think she knows something. We'll have to question her again. What else did you find?"

"The other women were also serviced by one person— Donald Cruz. There doesn't seem to be any repetition of the porters who cleaned the rooms. They're all different. There's also no indication that any of the lost jewelry has been found. You would think some of it would turn up if it was actually lost, but none has. The two constants are Acquino and Cruz."

"When we get back, let's interview Cruz," said Dave. "We'll see if he can come up with an answer as to why his patrons seem to be losing their jewelry. Maybe Eileen and Donald are working together. It's too much of a coincidence."

"That sounds like a good plan. But for now, let's forget about work and head over to Mama's Food Truck. I'm hungry. I could go for some Aruban pork chops with a side of plantains. I can smell them from here, and my mouth is watering. Let me finish my smoke first."

"I'm going to go for the Aruban steak with a side of fries,

and I'm going to share it with that gorgeous blond who's sunbathing topless by the water."

"Over Camille's dead body," said Pete.

While the Christoses were enjoying their day at Eagle Beach, Phillip had left the ship to locate Carib Jewelers in Aruba and cash in $40,000 worth of assorted diamond rings and earrings. But what Phillip didn't know was that Donald Cruz had also left the ship and was tailing him. Donald made sure he was always out of sight by hiding in the shadows of the trees and shrubs in a park across the street from Carib Jewelers. From there, he observed Phillip unseen.

When Phillip was done with his transactions, Donald waited for another fifteen minutes before he rose from his hiding place and entered the jewelry store. He wanted to make sure Phillip was long gone and on his way back to the ship. Donald had three diamond rings in a cloth. With those, he negotiated $15,000 for himself. He would not share this money. Instead, he would hide it in his suitcase with the rest of his stash. There was no way anyone could find out. As he happily walked back to the ship, he thought his actions were justified and that Eileen was a fool for not doing the same.

Meanwhile, Eileen was on the ship, breaking into more safes, but she wasn't happy about it. She was still slightly reeling from her encounter with Phillip the previous night. She had been startled by Phillip's behavior. She'd had no idea he could be such a bully or become so violent. She had seen no indication of it in the past. Phillip had always been such a likable and pleasant individual before. Eileen was a tough lady who feared no one, but she had to admit that she was shaken by his outburst. It was so out of character. She'd started to think that this ruse could not go on forever. At some point, the ship's security would get suspicious and investigate. They had to stop, or it would become obvious that the missing jewelry was not a coincidence. There had to be an endpoint, but Phillip seemed to think it could go on forever.

Eileen was becoming frightened by what she was doing. She had only been doing it several days, but she was tired of sneaking around and the danger of it all. She was also concerned about Pete and Dave Christos. They asked too many questions, and they seemed very smart. She didn't think they would quit until they had all the answers. Eileen was on edge. She was very careful, but she was afraid that she would make a silly mistake and reveal the whole plan. She didn't care about the money anymore. She had made thousands of dollars already. How much money did she need? She didn't want to do it anymore. She wanted out. She decided to tell Phillip that she wanted to quit. She didn't care if he flipped out, but she would have to wait. After their last meeting, they'd decided to cool off and skip a couple nights. They wouldn't meet again until after the boat left for Puerto Rico.

The next stop on the itinerary was Curacao, which—like Aruba—was known for its lovely beaches. Dave and Camille planned to go snorkeling. Pete and Lucia had signed up for the Curacao highlights tour, which would last four hours and included a stop for lunch. Curacao had been under Dutch rule until 2010. It was still part of the Netherlands but was an autonomous country. Pete and Lucia were adventurous eaters. They were glad the bus made a stop for lunch so that they could sample some of Curacao's cuisine.

As they disembarked from the bus, it was obvious that the national animal of Curacao was the iguana. They were ubiquitous. Pete and Lucia had to watch where they stepped because the iguanas were all over the sidewalks, climbing up poles, and in the streets. It wasn't surprising that iguana had become a common food in Curacao. It was prepared a number of ways, but the locals suggested that Pete and Lucia order something else with the iguana because it was very bony. It was an acquired taste that was not loved by all tourists, but Pete and Lucia planned to try it anyway. They were also looking forward to trying a Dutch snack called *bitterballen*, which was a ball of beef stew and gravy that was breaded, deep-fried, and served with mustard for dipping.

That night, when Pete, Lucia, Dave, and Camille got back on the ship, they went to a show and a specialty restaurant called the Beacon. It was an elegant restaurant that specialized in top-of-the-line seafood and meats. The four were able to choose from lobster, scallops, Dover sole, filet mignon, and rack of lamb. They ate their meals for free, courtesy of Captain Klein. After dinner, they headed over to the casino.

Since the next day would be a day at sea as the ship sailed to Old San Juan, Puerto Rico, Pete and Dave decided to dedicate the entire day to their investigation. They planned to meet with Captain Klein after they had questioned Donald Cruz and Eileen Acquino. They also wanted to visit the purser to see if there were any additional reports of lost jewelry. They were anticipating that their meeting with Captain Klein would help them come up with new strategies.

CHAPTER 10

The *Acme* was on its way to Puerto Rico, so Pete and Dave had work to do. They visited the purser after breakfast and found that there had been more lost jewelry reported in rooms serviced by Eileen Acquino and Donald Cruz. They got Cruz's number from the purser and gave him a call. He picked up immediately.

"Is this Donald Cruz, the butler?" asked Pete.

"Yes, who is this?" asked Donald.

"This is Pete Christos. My son, Dave, and I are both private investigators. We're investigating a rash of lost jewelry reported on this ship. My wife, Lucia, was one of the women who lost jewelry. She lost her diamond earrings, which were very valuable. We have some questions that we would like to ask you."

"Why do you want to ask me any questions? I don't even know your wife."

"We're looking for patterns, and it seems that half the women who have reported lost jewelry are serviced by you. We think that is highly unusual. We'd like to ask you about it."

"I'm sorry, but I'm very busy. My schedule is completely full. I can't find time to talk to you about it."

"Well find time!" Pete shouted. "Captain Klein has

asked me and Dave to look into this matter. If you don't cooperate, security will question you."

"OK, OK. When and where would you like to meet?"

"I'd like to meet now, in my room." Pete gave Donald the room number and hung up.

A few minutes later, Donald knocked on the door. Pete let him into the room and then sat on the sofa, next to Dave. The Christos men glared at Donald as he pulled out the desk chair and sat down. They were trying to intimidate him, and it was working. He appeared nervous.

"We've checked with the purser," said Dave. "They can track when butlers enter someone's room. On the days when the jewelry was lost, you were in those rooms. Can you explain why that is?"

"It's just a coincidence," said Donald. Beads of sweat appeared on his upper lip and forehead.

"Don't you think that's too much of a coincidence, Mr. Cruz?" Pete asked, raising his voice. "You went into those rooms and stole that jewelry, didn't you? How did you getting into those safes?"

"I'm not taking their jewelry, and I'm not getting into their safes. You know that's impossible. You're both crazy."

"Believe me, we're not crazy," said Dave. "We're very sane, and we're going to figure it out. Why do you appear so nervous? I see sweat above your brow and on your upper lip. I think you're guilty of something."

"I'm not guilty of anything. You're accusing me of something that I didn't do. Of course I'm nervous."

"So you think what's happening is just a coincidence?" asked Pete. "It's only you and one other butler that this is happening to. No other butlers seem to be involved. Don't you find that strange and troublesome? We do."

"Who's the other butler?" asked Donald.

"That's confidential," said Dave.

"Mr. Cruz, it appears that you are somehow involved in larceny," Pete said. "We don't have the proof yet, but we will find it. We have the cooperation of security and Captain Klein. We will be watching you from now on. You can go back to your duties."

Donald left the room, shaken. He'd never thought anyone would be suspicious. Things had appeared to be going so smoothly. He still had three stolen diamond rings that he wanted to keep for himself. He had planned to cash them in when he reached Puerto Rico. Now he would need to make sure nobody was tailing him when he got off the ship. He wasn't going to steal anymore jewelry if he was being watched.

It was late morning, so Pete and Dave decided to meet their wives for coffee and pastries before calling Eileen. As they ordered their cappuccinos and pastries, Lucia asked Pete how they were doing.

"We're doing very well. I think we are making progress.

Donald Cruz was sweating profusely when we questioned him. It's no coincidence that the jewelry only disappears from his and Eileen Acquino's rooms, not any other butlers'. It's obvious that the 'lost jewelry' was actually stolen. Even though it appears impossible, Eileen and Donald are somehow getting into the safes, stealing the jewelry, and probably selling it. But we have no proof. As of yet, there is no smoking gun."

"It makes me feel a little better, knowing I wasn't careless and didn't actually lose my earrings. What they're doing is horrible, especially because most of the jewelry were birthday or anniversary gifts. They have a special sentiment to the people. I hope you find that smoking gun soon and prove they're guilty."

"It's just a matter of time. We'll prove it, and you and the rest of the women can continue wearing your special jewelry without worry. We're going to call Eileen after we finish our pastries. She was very nervous the first time we questioned her. I think the cracks are forming. Maybe she'll completely break down this time.

After their coffee break, Pete and Dave went back to Pete's room and called Eileen Acquino.

"Eileen, this is Pete Christos. Dave and I would like you to come to my room."

"Again?" Eileen asked. "I thought you already asked me enough questions."

"Our investigation has uncovered new information that we'd like to ask you about. Could you come to my room now? Dave and I will be here. Let yourself in."

Eileen had barely survived their last round of questioning. What was the new information that they had found? As she approached Pete's room, she was suddenly sapped of strength, and her legs grew numb. She had to remain calm and under control. She knew Pete and Dave were predators, stalking their prey like wolverines. If they smelled blood, they would come in for the kill.

Eileen used her room card to enter the room. As she entered, Pete and Dave were sitting on the sofa. Both had pleasant smiles on their faces.

"Why don't you it on the desk chair and make yourself comfortable?" suggested Pete.

"You guys are starting to be a real pain in my ass, calling me in every day for questioning," said Eileen.

"You're going to see just how much of a pain in the ass we can be when you hear about the new information that we found," said Pete.

"I already told you what I do every day. I tend to my patrons' needs, deliver their snacks and wine in the afternoon, and fulfill any of their other special requests. That's it!"

"We've been meeting with the purser to see if there were any patterns with the lost jewelry," Pete said, "and it seems the involved women have the same butler—*you*. Actually, it was you and one other butler. We questioned him earlier this morning. He said it was just a coincidence, but we don't buy that."

"Who is the other butler?" asked Eileen.

"We can't divulge that information at this time," said Dave. "How can you account for so much of the lost jewelry being reported by women in rooms that you service? Much of the disappearances happened on your watch. That's very suspicious."

Pete and Dave had lost their smiles, and their intense eyes seemed to bore into Eileen's soul. She was unraveling.

"The purser can also track when butlers enter someone's room," Pete said. "You entered every patron's room on the days that their jewelry went missing. How do you account for that, Eileen?"

"I agree with the other butler," Eileen said. "It was a coincidence."

"We don't think so," said Dave, raising his voice. "We think you were somehow able to get into the safe and steal the jewelry."

Eileen teared up. "How could I possibly get in the safe?" The tears streaked down her cheeks.

"That's the one thing we can't figure out," Pete said, "but we definitely think you stole the jewelry. We've been detectives for a long time; we can feel when we're close to solving a case. It's a high for us. It's what we live for. We revel in it. It's like sniffing cocaine. We're almost there.

We have the cooperation of Captain Klein and the ship's security. It's just circumstantial evidence so far, but you're going to get careless. You and that other butler are going to make a mistake, and then we'll have you by the short hairs. We'll monitor you very closely, Eileen. You look nervous and upset, and I don't think those are tears of joy."

"I've just been accused of a crime that could put me away for many years. Of course I'm upset. I don't know what else to say."

"Nor do we have anything else to say, Eileen," said Dave. "You can go back to your duties, but don't be surprised if Captain Klein calls you in for a meeting."

Eileen left.

Dave looked to his Dad. "I thought she was going to fold. I think she's ready to give it up. The pressure's too much for her. But you're right—they're going to get careless and make a mistake. We're getting very close."

"Captain Klein wants us to report to her after lunch," Pete said, "so let's meet the wives at the Luminaire. I'm hungry after all that intense questioning."

CHAPTER 11

Pete and Dave met Captain Klein in her quarters at three o'clock. She wanted a report to see how they had progressed. The second in command was steering the ship to Puerto Rico while they met.

"So what have you found out so far?" Captain Klein asked. "Do you think you've made any progress?"

"We've questioned Eileen Acquino twice and Donald Cruz once," said Pete. "The purser was very helpful in tracking both of them and correlating the times when women lost their jewelry to the times when both of them entered the victim's rooms. There is no question that both of those butlers were in the rooms when the jewelry was lost. We have concluded that the jewelry was not lost but stolen; however, we can't figure out how those butlers were able to get into the safes."

"We have strict protocols for entering the safes. It's impossible for anyone to get in there, except for our special programmers."

"We know it's impossible," said Dave, "but it's the only logical explanation. Believe me—both of them are guilty. You should have seen the looks on their faces when we questioned them. We really let them have it. All the blood drained out of Cruz's face. He looked like a ghost. Eileen was literally shaking and in tears. They're guilty."

"The cruise is over in several more days," said Captain Klein. "I would like this case to be resolved as quickly as possible. As captain, I have the authority to question them and search their rooms. As detectives, what do you think I should do?"

"I think they are completely rattled," said Pete, "and I think they are going to do something really stupid that will reveal their subterfuge. Dave and I have been on so many cases where the culprits didn't know where to turn. They ran out of options and made fatal mistakes. They always wonder if they should stop what they're doing or continue. Then they make the wrong choice and get caught. I think we're at that juncture. Give us a couple more days, and you'll have all the evidence you need."

"I'm very impressed with your report and professionalism," Captain Klein said. "If we can keep this quiet and solve the case, it'll save me a lot of headaches. I'll give you a couple more days, but if nothing happens, security and I will interrogate them and search their rooms. This has been going on for far too long. We have to stop it. Keep me posted on any new developments, and thanks again."

After they finished their assignments for the day, Phillip, Donald, Eileen, and James met in Phillip's room.

"Did you know that Donald and I were questioned by Pete and Dave Christos today?" Eileen asked. "It's the second time I've been questioned by them. They are like predators stalking their prey. Apparently, Captain Klein asked the detectives to investigate the lost jewelry. They've found some damaging evidence. The pursers can track the butlers' movements and determine when they enter their assigned rooms. The detectives used this information to show that David and I were the only butlers with clients who lost jewelry. They figured out that we stole the jewelry. They accused both of us of theft, but they couldn't figure out how got into the safes. We're all sunk. I think we should stop altogether. Maybe they'll forget about it when their cruise is over and just go home. What do you think?"

"They questioned you and Donald, but they didn't question me or James."

"Gee, Phillip, thanks for your support," said Eileen.

"If you just keep your mouth shut about the phone app, we should be OK," said Phillip.

"I want out," said Eileen. "I'm scared shitless. I should have never gotten into this. What was I thinking?"

"You were greedy, just like the rest of us," Phillip said. "Look at all the money that you already have. I think we each have close to one hundred thousand dollars, especially after the additional money that I'm going to divide up tonight."

"All this money won't matter if we're behind bars," said Eileen.

"Maybe we should lay low for a while," James said. "We could not steal anymore jewelry. Phillip's right. They can't prove anything unless they have the phone app. I'm not going to say anything to anybody. I don't want to get caught and go to jail."

"OK, here's what I think we should do," Phillip said. "For the rest of this cruise, we just do our jobs. We don't take anymore jewelry. Then, at the start of the next cruise, we'll discuss what we want to do going forward. Maybe we can cut back on the people we steal from, so the frequency of lost jewelry looks more natural."

"You guys can do whatever you want, but I'm out of it," said Eileen. "My lips will stay sealed, but I don't want to be involved anymore. That's final!"

Phillip stared at Eileen for several seconds, trying to figure out whether or not he should be angry. Then he spoke. "Fine, you don't have to be part of this anymore. We can get someone else. But do I have to warn you what will happen if you talk?"

"Do we really have to go down this road again?" asked Eileen. "Between you and the Christos boys, I'm going to have to start carrying a gun."

"What about the two of you? Donald, James, are you still in?"

"I'm still in," they answered in unison.

Phillip said, "We will hold off on stealing more jewelry for the rest of the cruise. Do we all agree on that?"

They all nodded.

"Good. Let me divide up the rest of the money that I have here."

The next morning, the *Acme* docked in Old San Juan, Puerto Rico. Phillip was finally feeling relaxed. The pressure from running his scam and cashing in the stolen jewelry had taken its toll. He was usually a mild-mannered, pleasant, upbeat individual, but lately he'd had to control his temper and stop himself from snapping at people. He was relieved that his partners had agreed to stop stealing, at least for a while.

Phillip planned to get off the ship for a couple hours. He wanted to walk around Old San Juan and clear his head. As he strolled, he enjoyed the aromas of some of Puerto Rico's native dishes: *mofongo*, *tostones*, and *postelles*. He took his time sightseeing before he stopped for empanadas and a cold beer. He was feeling exuberant for the first time in ages.

Phillip was strolling down a busy promenade when he saw a sign for Carib Jewelers. Even though he had no jewelry to cash in, he decided to walk by, just to see where it was located for future reference. He had to walk down an alley to locate the store, which was situated in a small park and surrounded by lovely gardens. Phillip turned to the front of Carib Jewelers. Peeking inside the large window, Phillip saw

Donald Cruz. He was talking to a man who appeared to be the manager. Phillip backtracked, so he could spy on Donald unseen. What was Donald doing inside Carib Jewelers? He didn't have a girlfriend. Who was he buying jewelry for? As Phillip studied Donald through the window, his stream of consciousness kicked in. He visualized Donald going into a safe, taking the jewelry, and keeping it for himself. Phillip finally understood. Donald wasn't buying jewelry. He was cashing it in and keeping the money for himself.

Phillip became violently furious at Donald's betrayal. He would confront Donald when he came out of the store and walked down the alley. Phillip found a large brick on the pavement. He picked it up and hid in a doorway in the dark alley. Donald would have to pass him as he walked to the promenade. Phillip could not comprehend Donald's greed. How much money did he need? Phillip thought he'd been fair with his coconspirators. He'd divided the money equally, but this son of a bitch wanted more! It was never enough. Phillip was seething as he waited for Donald to walk by. He couldn't contain his fury.

When Donald had finally finished his business, he came out and turned into the alley. As Donald passed the doorway, Phillip darted out behind him and smashed him over the head with the brick. Unconscious, Donald fell to the pavement with a ghastly gash pulsating blood. Phillip reached down and took Donald's wallet, along with the large envelope that held the money. Then he ran away.

As Phillip ran away, a passerby saw Donald bleeding on the ground and yelled "El Alto." But Phillip was already at the promenade and lost in the crowd. The passerby called 911.

Phillip continued to run until he thought he was in the clear. His heart was thumping, and his breath came in short gasps. He sat on a bench to catch his breath. He had to get back to the ship by four o'clock, so he could help set up for the dinner rush at the buffet. As he sat on the bench and felt his heart flutter out of rhythm, the exuberance that he'd felt earlier turned to dread.

It was five o'clock, and the ship was ready to leave Old San Juan for the Dominican Republic. Whenever a ship was in port, the room card was used to record when a person disembarked from the ship and re-embarked. Everyone who left the ship—patrons and employees—was responsible for getting back on board before the ship left port. It was not the ship's responsibility to ensure everyone made it back on board, so if someone did not return in the allotted time, the ship left without them. Fifteen minutes prior to leaving, every ship would announce the names of the people who had not returned, in the hopes that they had somehow returned without showing their cards. Fifteen minutes prior to leaving for the Dominican Republic, only one name was announced.

"Donald Cruz, could you please call or report to the purser on level three?"

Pete, Dave, Lucia, and Camille were having cocktails outside, near the pool, when they heard the announcement.

"Cruz hasn't return to the boat yet?" asked Pete.

From their vantage point, they could see the gangplank and observe any late arrivals. No one was running to the ship.

"Maybe there was some mix up, and he's on the ship," said Dave. "Let's wait awhile and enjoy our cocktails."

Fifteen minutes after the ship left port, there was another announcement. "Donald Cruz, please call or report to the purser on level three."

"This doesn't sound good," Pete said. "Maybe Cruz left the ship and absconded with the money."

"But we still have Eileen," said Dave. "Maybe she knows something. Let's give Captain Klein a call and see what she thinks we should do."

CHAPTER 12

Eileen and Phillip were setting up the dinner buffet when they heard the announcement. Eileen felt like she'd experienced a horrible trauma. Her pulse quickened, and her breathing turned to short gasps. She felt nauseous and experienced some vertigo. She had to lean against a table to steady herself. *What did Donald do?* she thought to herself. *Did he escape with the money?* If he did, he was putting them all in jeopardy. It didn't make sense that he would do this. Eileen was certain she would be questioned again.

Phillip was working in another section of the buffet. Eileen walked over to him with an ashen face and asked, "Phillip, do you know anything? Did Donald get off the ship? Did he take off with the money? What's going on?"

"I don't know anything," Phillip said. "Just keep your mouth shut, and everything will be okay. Get back to work!"

When Pete's cell phone rang, it was Captain Klein calling. "Pete, I guess you heard the announcement. Donald Cruz did not return to the ship. What do you think that means?"

"The only conclusion that I can draw is that he took the money and is trying to avoid being caught," Pete said.

"That's what I thought. I'm done procrastinating. I want you and Dave to meet me at the purser's office on level three.

Then you, Dave, security, and I are going to go to Cruz's room below deck and search it for any clues as to what he might be doing. I'm also going to call Eileen Acquino down. I'd like to question her myself and search her room."

"Dave and I are on our way."

Eileen received the call from Captain Klein, instructing her to stop what she was doing and immediately report to her room for questioning. Eileen was in a daze. Her body felt hollow, like all her organs had been sucked out. She numbly took the elevator down to her room. There was nowhere to turn. She felt utterly helpless.

Captain Klein was able to access any room on the ship with her universal room card. She used it to access Donald Cruz's room. The room was tiny, so it wouldn't take long to search. There were two small bureaus, two small desks, two desk chairs, a television, and two twin-sized beds.

"Donald's roommate is Phillip Santos," Captain Klein said, "but I don't care. Search everything—the drawers, the luggage—everything."

They searched the bureaus and the desks to no avail. Then they ripped off the sheets and covers on the beds and turned over the mattresses. When they looked under the beds, they found two pieces of luggage.

"Open them," said Captain Klein.

Pete opened one of the suitcases, and Dave opened the other. Inside were hundreds of one-hundred-dollar bills.

"I'll be damned," said Pete.

"There must be one hundred thousand dollars in each suitcase," Dave said. "It looks like Phillip was also involved."

"Security, I want you to find Phillip Santos and march him down here," said Captain Klein. "Eileen should be in her room by now. Let's go!"

They left the room and walked to Eileen's room. Captain Klein knocked on Eileen's door. When Eileen opened the door, she was already in tears. She looked utterly broken.

"We found money in Donald Cruz's room, in his suitcase," Captain Klein said. "Phillip's suitcase had the same amount of money. I assume all of you were part of the same scam. Where's your suitcase, Eileen?"

"It's under the bed. The money's inside," said Eileen.

"I don't understand why Donald's money is still on the ship," said Pete. "I would've thought he would take the money with him if he was trying to escape."

"I don't know anything about that," said Eileen. "Phillip is Donald's roommate. Why don't you ask him?"

Captain Klein said, "We're going to have to report this to the FBI. If you give us some information, maybe the authorities will go a little easier on you."

"I'll tell you anything you want to know," said Eileen.

Security knocked on the door. Then they and Phillip entered the room.

"Phillip, you were always singing and putting everyone in a good mood," said Pete. "I can't believe you're part of this. When we searched Donald's room, we found almost one hundred thousand dollars in your suitcase. Can you explain that?"

Phillip stood there, mute.

Pete continued, "Don't be afraid to talk, Phillip. You are guilty of stealing the jewelry, along with your compatriots. But here's what I don't understand. If Donald was trying to get away, why did he leave his money here?"

"It looks like we're not going to get much information from Phillip," said Dave.

"Maybe Eileen will be more cooperative," Pete said. "Now we're coming in for the kill. This part of the mystery, we couldn't solve. How did you get into the safes?"

"Get Phillip's phone, and give it to me," said Eileen.

Dave had to wrestle the phone from Phillip. Once he had it, he gave it to Eileen.

"Phillip has an app on his phone," Eileen said while clicking open the app. "I'm going to place the phone against my safe. Look at the screen."

The numbers seven, six, one, three appeared on the screen.

"That's the combination to my safe," said Eileen.

Phillip lunged toward Eileen in anger, and security had to restrain him.

"Oh my god!" said Captain Klein.

"We could go into any room and access the safe's combination," said Eileen. "Then we'd open the safe and take the jewelry. If we were smarter, it could have gone on forever."

"If we didn't find this out, it could've ruined the cruise industry," said Captain Klein.

"Where did you get this app, Phillip?" asked Pete. "Is it something that you developed? Come on; start to talk. There's no way you're getting away with this. Help us, and maybe the authorities will give you a break."

Phillip flopped down on the bed, thinking for a moment. He knew Pete was right. The only way he would benefit from this was by giving them information. Eventually, he said, "OK, I know I'm screwed, so I'll cooperate. I have a friend back in Quezon City who developed this technology and invented the app. He's a computer geek. He wanted me to test it while on the ship. I was shocked and amazed to see that it worked, so I showed it to Donald. I needed someone who could get into the rooms, access the safe's combination, and take the jewelry. Donald was perfect for the job. Since he was a butler, he could get into his patrons' rooms whenever he wanted.

"I came up with a plan to target expensive jewelry. We focused on the casino, because women love to wear their expensive jewelry and show it off there. While I was in the casino, taking drink orders, I observed what women were wearing expensive jewelry. I would take their drink orders and their room cards to the bartender. Giving him a prearranged signal, I would indicate what rooms were targets. When he saw the signal, he would write the room numbers on a separate piece of paper. If any of the rooms were serviced by Donald, he would steal the jewelry."

"Sounds like a great plan. It's a shame you got caught," said Dave.

"You're a real ball buster, aren't you?" asked Phillip.

"How did Eileen fit in?" asked Captain Klein.

Phillip said, "The plan was working so well that I asked Donald to recruit anther butler. He suggested Eileen. Even though I'm very pissed at her now, I must admit that she did an excellent job."

Who is the bartender?" asked Captain Klein.

"James Mendoza," said Phillip.

Captain Klein said, "We're going to question Mendoza as soon as we're through with the both of you. Was anyone else involved?"

"No, it was just the four of us. I divided the money equally among the four of us."

"How did you cash in the jewelry?" asked Dave.

"I found a jewelry company that would buy stolen jewelry. It's called Carib Jewelers. It has outlets all over the islands. I would get off the ship on port days and receive cash for the stolen jewelry."

"Well, we know that there are four coconspirators," said Pete, "but we only have three on the ship. Where's the fourth? Where's Donald Cruz? Are you sure you don't know where he went, Phillip? You're his roommate."

Phillip bowed his head bowed. He was feeling a great deal of remorse and shame as his eyes welled up with tears. "Sometimes my anger gets the best of me. Sometimes it's almost uncontrollable. I left the ship in Puerto Rico, for a couple hours of R and R. I was feeling relieved because the team had decided to stop stealing jewelry for the rest of the cruise. I was strolling around Old San Juan, enjoying the sights when, on a whim, I thought to check out Carib Jewelers for future reference. When I got to the jewelers, I saw Donald inside. It dawned on me that Donald was stealing jewelry and cashing it in for himself—not sharing with the rest of us. I became violently angry, so I hid in a doorway in the alley. I found a large brick on the pavement. When Donald passed me, I darted out behind him and smashed him over the head. Then took his money and ran away. I'm sorry. I don't know where he is or if he's dead or alive." As he finished speaking, Phillip began to sob.

"Well, I have a lot of work to do," said Captain Klein. "I'm going to have to alert the FBI and tell them about that phone app. If they can't track down Phillip's buddy in Quezon City and find a way to neutralize or destroy the app, it'll have a disastrous effect on the cruise industry. I'll also see if they can locate Donald Cruz in Puerto Rico. We're done questioning the two of you. I'll get ahold of James Mendoza. When we get to the Dominican Republic, the FBI will take over. I'll give them all this money, and hopefully, they'll be able to distribute it back to the affected parties."

"Is there anything else you want us to do?" asked Pete.

Captain Klein said, "No, but I want to thank you both profusely for the work that you've done. If it weren't for the two of you, we would have never solved this case. I'm forever in your debt. I want you to enjoy the last several days of your cruise. Make sure you take advantage of our specialty restaurants."

"We will definitely do that," said Pete.

EPILOGUE

The Christoses were in high spirits after returning from their vacation. They had thoroughly enjoyed their wonderful cruise and taken full advantage of the ship's amenities and specialty restaurants, which had been comped by Captain Klein. They loved displaying the bronze tans that they had acquired while on vacation, making them the envy of all their colleagues in Burlington, Vermont. They also took satisfaction in helping solve a case that could have been devastating to the cruise industry. If the participants had not been so greedy, many other women would have been victims, losing their jewelry.

The newspapers and major cable networks all reported the exploits of Pete and Dave Christos. They were both interviewed, where they explained the sequence of events and how they had used their powers of deductive reasoning to solve the case. They had been labeled the "Cruise Detectives." The *Burlington Free Journal* in ran a front-page feature article about the case, adding to the detective agency's notoriety, as well as gaining business for Lucia and Camille's travel agency. Pete and Dave became celebrities. Everything about the cruise turned out positive.

It had the opposite outcome for Phillip Santos, Donald Cruz, Eileen Acquino, and James Mendoza. The FBI was able to track down Donald Cruz at San Juan City Hospital. He had been transported there by the local police and placed in the trauma unit. After sustaining the serious head injury, he had been in a coma for several days. He came out of the coma and fully recovered within ten days, but to his chagrin, he was taken into custody after being released from the hospital. The other three culprits were also taken into custody, and all were awaiting trial. They could expect to spend many years in jail for perpetuating the scam.

Phillip Santos was extensively questioned about his phone app by the FBI. His computer friend liked to tinker with technology. He had invented the phone app, but he never intended to use it. He knew Phillip worked on a cruise ship, where virtually every room had a safe, so he'd asked Phillip to test the app. He was just curious to see if it would work. It was Phillip's idea to steal the jewelry. The computer geek knew nothing about Phillip's plan. Unfortunately, he was still an accessory and would also face jail time.

Captain Klein had reported the crime to the cruise company. In her report, she praised Pete and Dave Christos for their comprehensive detective work and emphasized the fact that the case could not have been solved without them. The detectives and their wives were awarded a free cruise with two suites, and their future meals at the ship's specialty restaurants would be comped. They were also given 50 percent discount on all future cruises. To further show their appreciation, each member of the Christos family received

$1,000 to be used at the casino. It was the least that the cruise company could do for the Christoses, since they had virtually saved the cruise industry.

Pete, Lucia, Dave, and Camille met at the Hen of the Wood, a restaurant inside the Hotel Vermont. There, they rehashed their vacation while they selected items from the menu. Because Lucia's expensive earrings had been stolen, she would receive $1,000 from the FBI. Each woman who'd had their jewelry stolen would receive a similar amount.

The Christoses talked about all the amenities on the cruise and about their interesting excursions. They couldn't wait for the next free cruise, which would be to the Mediterranean. Free airfare had been included in the deal. They also talked about the case and its participants—Phillip Santos, Donald Cruz, Eileen Acquino, and James Mendoza. They agreed that it was a master plot.

As they were finishing their dessert, Pete mad a cogent observation. "As detectives who have been involved in so many cases, we should have known it all along."

"What was that, Dad?"

"The butler did it!"